Edward
goes to the woods

Illustrated by Peter Lawson
Series editor: Teresa Wilson

Published in Great Britain in 2002 by Egmont Books Limited,
239 Kensington High Street, London, W8 6SA
Printed in Italy
ISBN 0 7498 5488 X

10 9 8 7 6 5 4 3 2 1

Educational consultant: Betty Root, formerly Director of the Reading Centre in the University of Reading.

Edward puffed slowly through the woods.

"The trees look lovely, don't they?"
he said to the driver.

"Soon it will be winter and the leaves
will fall off," the driver told him.

"I hope they won't," said Edward.

Children ran along the field
by the track.

Edward laughed as they
waved to him.

When he got back, The Fat Controller was waiting for him.

"It was lovely down in the woods," said Edward.
"And we saw lots of children."

"I'll come with you tomorrow and you can show me your lovely woods," said The Fat Controller.

"And the red and yellow leaves," said Edward.

That night the wind began to blow.

"The wind is keeping me awake," said Edward.

It kept all the engines awake.

The next day, Edward said, "I don't like the wind. It makes my eyes hurt."

"It blows my hair about," said Bridget.

"Not mine!" laughed The Fat Controller.

"Let's go and see your lovely woods," said Bridget.

The Fat Controller and Bridget got into the coach and Edward moved slowly off.

15

The wind blew so hard that Edward couldn't keep his eyes open.

The leaves from the trees flew up into the sky.

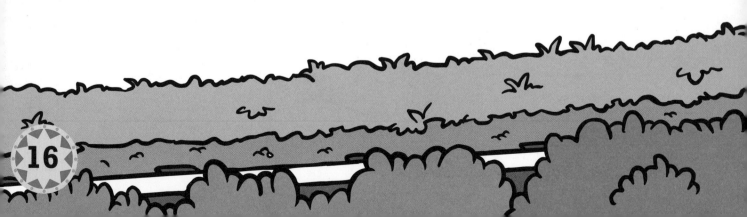

When they got into the woods, all the leaves had blown off the trees.

"Oh dear," said Edward.
"Look at my lovely woods now."

When Edward stopped, Bridget and The Fat Controller got out of the coach.

"Oh, this is lovely," said Bridget, as she kicked the leaves into the air.
"Can we stay here all day?" she asked.

"Of course we can," said The Fat Controller.
"I think it looks just as lovely with the leaves on the ground."

But Edward wasn't pleased.

"I'm sorry you didn't see the trees with their red and yellow leaves on," he said.

"Never mind," laughed The Fat Controller looking at Edward.

"It was worth it just to see you covered in leaves."

"Now you look like one of the trees too!"
said Bridget, and they all laughed.